THE INCONSIDERATE WAITER

THE INCONSIDERATE WAITER

J. M. BARRIE

WILDSIDE PRESS

COPYRIGHT INFORMATION

Published by Wildside Press LLC.
www.wildsidebooks.com

CHAPTER

Frequently I have to ask myself in the street for the name of the man I bowed to just now, and then, before I can answer, the wind of the first corner blows him from my memory. I have a theory, however, that those puzzling faces, which pass before I can see who cut the coat, all belong to club waiters.

Until William forced his affairs upon me that was all I did know of the private life of waiters, though I have been in the club for twenty years. I was even unaware whether they slept downstairs or had their own homes; nor had I the interest to inquire of other members, nor they the knowledge to inform me. I hold that this sort of people should be fed and clothed and given airing and wives and children, and I subscribe yearly, I believe for these purposes; but to come into closer relation with waiters is bad form; they are club fittings, and William should have kept his distress to himself, or taken it away and patched it up like a rent in one of the chairs. His inconsiderateness has been a pair of spectacles to me for months.

It is not correct taste to know the name of a club waiter, so I must apologise for knowing William's, and still more for not forgetting it. If, again, to speak of a waiter is bad form, to speak bitterly is the comic degree of it. But William has disappointed me sorely. There were years when I would defer dining several minutes that he might wait on me. His pains to reserve the window-seat for me were perfectly satisfactory. I allowed him privileges, as to suggest dishes, and would give him information, as that some one had startled me in the reading-room by slamming a door. I have shown him how I cut my finger with a piece of string. Obviously he was gratified by these attentions, usually recommending a liqueur; and I fancy he must have understood my sufferings, for he often looked ill himself. Probably he was rheumatic, but I cannot say for certain, as I never thought of asking, and he had the sense to see that the knowledge would be offensive to me.

In the smoking-room we have a waiter so independent that once, when he brought me a yellow chartreuse, and I said I had ordered green, he replied, "No, sir; you said yellow." William could never have been guilty of such effrontery. In appearance, of course, he is mean, but I can no more describe him than a milkmaid could draw cows. I suppose we distinguish one waiter from another much as we pick our hat from the rack. We could have plotted a murder safely before William. He never presumed to have any opinions of his own. When such was my mood he remained silent, and if I announced that something diverting had happened to me he laughed before I told him what it was. He turned the twinkle in his eye off or on at my bidding as readily as if it was the gas. To my "Sure to be wet to-morrow," he would reply, "Yes, sir;" and to Trelawney's "It doesn't look like rain," two minutes afterward, he would reply, "No, sir." It was one member who said Lightning Rod would win the Derby and another who said Lightning Rod had no chance, but it was William who agreed with both. He was like a cheroot, which may be smoked from either end. So used was I to him that, had he died or got another situation (or whatever it is such persons do when they disappear from the club), I should probably have told the head waiter to bring him back, as I disliked changes.

It would not become me to know precisely when I began to think William an ingrate, but I date his lapse from the evening when he brought me oysters. I detest oysters, and no one knew it better than William. He has agreed with me that he could not understand any gentleman's liking them. Between me and a certain member who smacks his lips twelve times to a dozen of them William knew I liked a screen to be placed until we had reached the soup, and yet he gave me the oysters and the other man my sardine. Both the other member and I quickly called for brandy and the head waiter. To do William justice, he shook, but never can I forget his audacious explanation: "Beg pardon, sir, but I was thinking of something else."

In these words William had flung off the mask, and now I knew him for what he was.

I must not be accused of bad form for looking at William on the following evening. What prompted me to do so was not personal interest in him, but a desire to see whether I dare let him wait on me again. So, recalling that a caster was off a chair yesterday, one is entitled to make sure that it is on to-day before sitting down. If the expression is not too strong, I may say that I was taken aback by William's manner. Even when crossing the room to take my orders he let his one hand play nervously with the other. I had to repeat "Sardine on toast" twice, and instead of answering "Yes, sir," as if my selection of sardine on toast was a personal gratification to him, which is the manner one expects of a waiter, he glanced at the clock, then out at the window, and, starting, asked, "Did you say sardine on toast, sir?"

It was the height of summer, when London smells like a chemist's shop, and he who has the dinner-table at the window needs no candles to show him his knife and fork. I lay back at intervals, now watching a starved-looking woman sleep on a door-step, and again complaining of the club bananas. By-and-by I saw a girl of the commonest kind, ill-clad and dirty, as all these Arabs are. Their parents should be compelled to feed and clothe them comfortably, or at least to keep them indoors, where they cannot offend our eyes. Such children are for pushing aside with one's umbrella; but this girl I noticed because she was gazing at the club windows. She had stood thus for perhaps ten minutes when I became aware that some one was leaning over me to look out at the window. I turned round. Conceive my indignation on seeing that the rude person was William.

"How dare you, William?" I said, sternly. He seemed not to hear me. Let me tell, in the measured words of one describing a past incident, what then took place. To get nearer the window he pressed heavily on my shoulder.

"William, you forget yourself!" I said, meaning—as I see now—that he had forgotten me.

I heard him gulp, but not to my reprimand. He was scanning the street. His hands chattered on my shoulder, and, pushing him from me, I saw that his mouth was agape.

"What are you looking for?" I asked.

He stared at me, and then, like one who had at last heard the echo of my question, seemed to be brought back to the club. He turned his face from me for an instant, and answered shakily:

"I beg your pardon, sir! I—I shouldn't have done it. Are the bananas too ripe, sir?"

He recommended the nuts, and awaited my verdict so anxiously while I ate one that I was about to speak graciously, when I again saw his eyes drag him to the window.

"William," I said, my patience giving way at last, "I dislike being waited on by a melancholy waiter."

"Yes, sir," he replied, trying to smile, and then broke out passionately, "For God's sake, sir, tell me, have you seen a little girl looking in at the club windows?"

He had been a good waiter once, and his distracted visage was spoiling my dinner.

"There," I said, pointing to the girl, and no doubt would have added that he must bring me coffee immediately, had he continued to listen. But already he was beckoning to the child. I have not the least interest in her (indeed, it had never struck me that waiters had private affairs, and I still think it a pity that they should have); but as I happened to be looking out at the window I could not avoid seeing what occurred. As soon as the girl saw William she ran into the street, regardless of vehicles, and nodded three times to him. Then she disappeared.

I have said that she was quite a common child, without attraction of any sort, and yet it was amazing the difference she made in William. He gasped relief, like one who had broken through the anxiety that checks breathing, and into his face there came a silly laugh of happiness. I had dined well, on the whole, so I said:

"I am glad to see you cheerful again, William."

I meant that I approved his cheerfulness because it helped my digestion, but he must needs think I was sympathising with him.

"Thank you, sir," he answered. "Oh, sir! when she nodded and I saw it was all right I could have gone down on my knees to God."

I was as much horrified as if he had dropped a plate on my toes. Even William, disgracefully emotional as he was at the moment, flung out his arms to recall the shameful words.

"Coffee, William!" I said, sharply.

I sipped my coffee indignantly, for it was plain to me that William had something on his mind.

"You are not vexed with me, sir?" he had the hardihood to whisper.

"It was a liberty," I said.

"I know, sir; but I was beside myself."

"That was a liberty also."

He hesitated, and then blurted out:

"It is my wife, sir. She—"

I stopped him with my hand. William, whom I had favoured in so many ways, was a married man! I might have guessed as much years before had I ever reflected about waiters, for I knew vaguely that his class did this sort of thing. His confession was distasteful to me, and I said warningly:

"Remember where you are, William."

"Yes, sir; but you see, she is so delicate—"

"Delicate! I forbid your speaking to me on unpleasant topics."

"Yes, sir; begging your pardon."

It was characteristic of William to beg my pardon and withdraw his wife, like some unsuccessful dish, as if its taste would not remain in the mouth. I shall be chided for questioning him further about his wife, but, though doubtless an unusual step, it was only bad form superficially, for my motive was irreproachable. I inquired for his wife, not because I was interested in her welfare, but in the hope of allaying my irritation. So I am entitled to invite the wayfarer who has bespattered me with mud to scrape it off.

I desired to be told by William that the girl's signals meant his wife's recovery to health. He should have seen that such was my wish and answered accordingly. But, with the brutal inconsiderateness of his class, he said:

"She has had a good day; but the doctor, he—the doctor is afeard she is dying."

Already I repented my questions. William and his wife seemed in league against me, when they might so easily have chosen some other member.

"Pooh! the doctor," I said.

"Yes, sir," he answered.

"Have you been married long, William?"

"Eight years, sir. Eight years ago she was—I—I mind her when . . . and now the doctor says—"

The fellow gaped at me. "More coffee, sir?" he asked.

"What is her ailment?"

"She was always one of the delicate kind, but full of spirit, and—and you see, she has had a baby lately—"

"William!"

"And she—I—the doctor is afeard she's not picking up."

"I feel sure she will pick up."

"Yes, sir?"

It must have been the wine I had drunk that made me tell him:

"I was once married, William. My wife—it was just such a case as yours."

"She did not get better sir?"

"No."

After a pause he said, "Thank you, sir," meaning for the sympathy that made me tell him that. But it must have been the wine.

"That little girl comes here with a message from your wife?"

"Yes; if she nods three times it means my wife is a little better."

"She nodded thrice to-day."

"But she is told to do that to relieve me, and maybe those nods don't tell the truth."

"Is she your girl?"

"No; we have none but the baby. She is a neighbour's; she comes twice a day."

"It is heartless of her parents not to send her every hour."

"But she is six years old," he said, "and has a house and two sisters to look after in the daytime, and a dinner to cook. Gentlefolk don't understand."

"I suppose you live in some low part, William."

"Off Drury Lane," he answered, flushing; "but—but it isn't low. You see, we were never used to anything better, and I mind when I let her see the house before we were married, she—she a sort of cried because she was so proud of it. That was eight years ago, and now—she's afeard she'll die when I'm away at my work."

"Did she tell you that?"

"Never; she always says she is feeling a little stronger."

"Then how can you know she is afraid of that?"

"I don't know how I know, sir; but when I am leaving the house in the morning I look at her from the door, and she looks at me, and then I—I know."

"A green chartreuse, William!"

I tried to forget William's vulgar story in billiards, but he had spoiled my game. My opponent, to whom I can give twenty, ran out when I was sixty-seven, and I put aside my cue pettishly. That in itself was bad form, but what would they have thought had they known that a waiter's impertinence caused it! I grew angrier with William as the night wore on, and next day I punished him by giving my orders through another waiter.

As I had my window-seat, I could not but see that the girl was late again. Somehow I dawdled over my coffee. I had an evening paper before me, but there was so little in it that my eyes found more of interest in the street. It did not matter to me whether William's wife died, but when that girl had promised to come, why did she not come? These lower classes only give their word to break it. The coffee was undrinkable.

At last I saw her. William was at another window, pretending to do something with the curtains. I stood up, pressing closer to the window. The coffee had been so bad that I felt shaky. She nodded three times, and smiled.

"She is a little better," William whispered to me, almost gaily.

"Whom are you speaking of?" I asked, coldly, and immediately retired to the billiard-room, where I played a capital game. The coffee was much better there than in the dining-room.

Several days passed, and I took care to show William that I had forgotten his maunderings. I chanced to see the little girl (though I never looked for her) every evening, and she always nodded three times, save once, when she shook her head, and then William's face grew white as a napkin. I remember this incident because that night I could not get into a pocket. So badly did I play that the thought of it kept me awake in bed, and that, again, made me wonder how William's wife was. Next day I went to the club early (which was not my custom) to see the new books. Being in the club at any rate, I looked into the dining-room to ask William if I had left my gloves there, and the sight of him reminded me of his wife; so I asked for her. He shook his head mournfully, and I went off in a rage.

So accustomed am I to the club that when I dine elsewhere I feel uncomfortable next morning, as if I had missed a dinner. William knew this; yet here he was, hounding me out of the club! That evening I dined (as the saying is) at a restaurant, where no sauce was served with the asparagus. Furthermore, as if that were not triumph enough for William, his doleful face came between me and every dish, and I seemed to see his wife dying to annoy me.

I dined next day at the club for self-preservation, taking, however, a table in the middle of the room, and engaging a waiter who had once nearly poisoned me by not interfering when I put two lumps of sugar into my coffee instead of one, which is my allowance. But no William came to me to acknowledge his humiliation, and by-and-by I became aware that he was not in the room. Suddenly the thought struck me that his wife must be dead, and I—It was the worst cooked and the worst served dinner I ever had in the club.

I tried the smoking-room. Usually the talk there is entertaining, but on that occasion it was so frivolous that I did not remain five minutes. In the card-room a member told me excitedly that a policeman had spoken rudely to him; and my strange comment was:

"After all, it is a small matter."

In the library, where I had not been for years, I found two members asleep, and, to my surprise, William on a ladder dusting books.

"You have not heard, sir?" he said, in answer to my raised eyebrows. Descending the ladder, he whispered tragically: "It was last evening, sir. I—I lost my head, and I—swore at a member."

I stepped back from William, and glanced apprehensively at the two members. They still slept.

"I hardly knew," William went on, "what I was doing all day yesterday, for I had left my wife so weakly that—"

I stamped my foot.

"I beg your pardon for speaking of her," he had the grace to say, "but I couldn't help slipping up to the window often yesterday to look for Jenny, and when she did come, and I saw she was crying, it—it sort of confused me, and I didn't know right, sir, what I was doing. I hit against a member, Mr. Myddleton Finch, and he—he jumped and swore at me. Well, sir, I had just touched him after all, and I was so miserable, it a kind of stung me to be treated like—like that, and me a man as well as him; and I lost my senses, and—and I swore back."

William's shamed head sank on his chest, but I even let pass his insolence in likening himself to a member of the club, so afraid was I of the sleepers waking and detecting me in talk with a waiter.

"For the love of God," William cried, with coarse emotion, "don't let them dismiss me!"

"Speak lower!" I said. "Who sent you here?"

"I was turned out of the dining-room at once, and told to attend to the library until they had decided what to do with me. Oh, sir, I'll lose my place!"

He was blubbering, as if a change of waiters, was a matter of importance.

"This is very bad, William," I said. "I fear I can do nothing for you."

"Have mercy on a distracted man!" he entreated. "I'll go on my knees to Mr. Myddleton Finch."

How could I but despise a fellow who would be thus abject for a pound a week?

"I dare not tell her," he continued, "that I have lost my place. She would just fall back and die."

"I forbade your speaking of your wife," I said, sharply, "unless you can speak pleasantly of her."

"But she may be worse now, sir, and I cannot even see Jenny from here. The library windows look to the back."

"If she dies," I said, "it will be a warning to you to marry a stronger woman next time."

Now every one knows that there is little real affection among the lower orders. As soon as they have lost one mate they take another. Yet William, forgetting our relative positions, drew himself up and raised his fist, and if I had not stepped back I swear he would have struck me.

The highly improper words William used I will omit, out of consideration for him. Even while he was apologising for them I retired to the smoking-room, where I found the cigarettes so badly rolled that they would not keep alight. After a little I remembered that I wanted to see Myddleton Finch about an improved saddle of which a friend of his has the patent. He was in the newsroom, and, having questioned him about the saddle, I said:

"By the way, what is this story about your swearing at one of the waiters?"

"You mean about his swearing at me," Myddleton Finch replied, reddening.

"I am glad that was it," I said; "for I could not believe you guilty of such bad form."

"If I did swear—" he was beginning, but I went on:

"The version which has reached me was that you swore at him, and he repeated the word. I heard he was to be dismissed and you reprimanded."

"Who told you that?" asked Myddleton Finch, who is a timid man.

"I forget; it is club talk," I replied, lightly. "But of course the committee will take your word. The waiter, whichever one he is, richly deserves his dismissal for insulting you without provocation."

Then our talk returned to the saddle, but Myddleton Finch was abstracted, and presently he said:

"Do you know, I fancy I was wrong in thinking that the waiter swore at me, and I'll withdraw my charge to-morrow."

Myddleton Finch then left me, and, sitting alone, I realised that I had been doing William a service. To some slight extent I may have intentionally helped him to retain his place in the club, and I now see the reason, which was that he alone knows precisely to what extent I like my claret heated.

For a mere second I remembered William's remark that he should not be able to see the girl Jenny from the library windows. Then this recollection drove from my head that I had only dined in the sense that my dinner-bill was paid. Returning to the dining-room, I happened to take my chair at the window, and while I was eating a deviled kidney I saw in the street the girl whose nods had such an absurd effect on William.

The children of the poor are as thoughtless as their parents, and this Jenny did not sign to the windows in the hope that William might see her, though she could not see him. Her face, which was disgracefully dirty, bore doubt and dismay on it, but whether she brought good news it would not tell. Somehow I had expected her to signal when she saw me, and, though her message could not interest me, I was in the mood in which one is irritated at that not taking place which he is awaiting. Ultimately she seemed to be making up her mind to go away.

A boy was passing with the evening papers, and I hurried out to get one, rather thoughtlessly, for we have all the papers in the club.

Unfortunately, I misunderstood the direction the boy had taken; but round the first corner (out of sight of the club windows) I saw the girl Jenny, and so asked her how William's wife was.

"Did he send you to me?" she replied, impertinently taking me for a waiter. "My!" she added, after a second scrutiny, "I b'lieve you're one of them. His missis is a bit better, and I was to tell him as she took all the tapiocar."

"How could you tell him?" I asked.

"I was to do like this," she replied, and went through the supping of something out of a plate in dumb-show.

"That would not show she ate all the tapioca," I said.

"But I was to end like this," she answered, licking an imaginary plate with her tongue.

I gave her a shilling (to get rid of her), and returned to the club disgusted.

Later in the evening I had to go to the club library for a book, and while William was looking in vain for it (I had forgotten the title) I said to him:

"By the way, William, Mr. Myddleton Finch is to tell the committee that he was mistaken in the charge he brought against you, so you will doubtless be restored to the dining-room to-morrow."

The two members were still in their chairs, probably sleeping lightly; yet he had the effrontery to thank me.

"Don't thank me," I said, blushing at the imputation. "Remember your place, William!"

"But Mr. Myddleton Finch knew I swore," he insisted.

"A gentleman," I replied, stiffly, "cannot remember for twenty-four hours what a waiter has said to him."

"No, sir; but—"

To stop him I had to say: "And, ah, William, your wife is a little better. She has eaten the tapioca—all of it."

"How can your know, sir?"

"By an accident."

"Jenny signed to the window?"

"No."

"Then you saw her, and went out, and—"

"Nonsense!"

"Oh, sir, to do that for me! May God bl—"

"William!"

"Forgive me, sir; but—when I tell my missis, she will say it was thought of your own wife as made you do it."

He wrung my hand. I dared not withdraw it, lest we should waken the sleepers.

William returned to the dining-room, and I had to show him that if he did not cease looking gratefully at me I must change my waiter. I also ordered him to stop telling me nightly how his wife was, but I continued to know, as I could not help seeing the girl Jenny from the window. Twice in a week I learned from this objectionable child that the ailing woman had again eaten all the tapioca. Then I became suspicious of William. I will tell why.

It began with a remark of Captain Upjohn's. We had been speaking of the inconvenience of not being able to get a hot dish served after 1 A.M., and he said:

"It is because these lazy waiters would strike. If the beggars had a love of their work they would not rush away from the club the moment one o'clock strikes. That glum fellow who often waits on you takes to his heels the moment he is clear of the club steps. He ran into me the other night at the top of the street, and was off without apologising."

"You mean the foot of the street, Upjohn," I said; for such is the way to Drury Lane.

"No; I mean the top. The man was running west."

"East."

"West."

I smiled, which so annoyed him that he bet me two to one in sovereigns. The bet could have been decided most quickly by asking William a question, but I thought, foolishly doubtless, that it might hurt his feelings, so I watched him leave the club. The possibility of Upjohn's winning the bet had seemed remote to me. Conceive my surprise, therefore when William went westward.

Amazed, I pursued him along two streets without realising that I was doing so. Then curiosity put me into a hansom. We followed William, and it proved to be a three-shilling fare, for, running when he was in breath and walking when he was out of it, he took me to West Kensington.

I discharged my cab, and from across the street watched William's incomprehensible behaviour. He had stopped at a dingy row of workmen's houses, and knocked at the darkened window of one of them. Presently a light showed. So far as I could see, some one pulled up the blind and for ten minutes talked to William. I was uncertain whether they talked, for the window was not opened, and I felt that, had William spoken through the glass loud enough to be heard inside, I must have heard him too. Yet he nodded and beckoned. I was still bewildered when, by setting off the way he had come, he gave me the opportunity of going home.

Knowing from the talk of the club what the lower orders are, could I doubt that this was some discreditable love-affair of William's? His solicitude for his wife had been mere pretence; so far as it was genuine, it meant that he feared she might recover. He probably told her that he was detained nightly in the club till three.

I was miserable next day, and blamed the deviled kidneys for it. Whether William was unfaithful to his wife was nothing to me, but I had two plain reasons for insisting on his going straight home from his club: the one that, as he had made me lose a bet, I must punish him; the other that he could wait upon me better if he went to bed betimes.

Yet I did not question him. There was something in his face that—Well, I seemed to see his dying wife in it.

I was so out of sorts that I could eat no dinner. I left the club. Happening to stand for some time at the foot of the street, I chanced to see the girl Jenny coming, and—No; let me tell the truth, though the whole club reads: I was waiting for her.

"How is William's wife to-day?" I asked.

"She told me to nod three times," the little slattern replied; "but she looked like nothink but a dead one till she got the brandy.

"Hush, child!" I said, shocked. "You don't know how the dead look."

"Bless yer," she answered, "don't I just! Why, I've helped to lay 'em out. I'm going on seven."

"Is William good to his wife?"

"Course he is. Ain't she his missis?"

"Why should that make him good to her?" I asked, cynically, out of my knowledge of the poor. But the girl, precocious in many ways, had never had any opportunities of studying the lower classes in the newspapers, fiction, and club talk. She shut one eye, and, looking up wonderingly, said:

"Ain't you green—just!"

"When does William reach home at night?"

"'Tain't night; it's morning. When I wakes up at half dark and half light, and hears a door shutting, I know as it's either father going off to his work or Mr. Hicking come home from his."

"Who is Mr. Hicking?"

"Him as we've been speaking on—William. We calls him mister, 'cause he's a toff. Father's just doing jobs in Covent Gardens, but Mr. Hicking, he's a waiter, and a clean shirt every day. The old woman would like father to be a waiter, but he hain't got the 'ristocratic look."

"What old woman?"

"Go 'long! that's my mother. Is it true there's a waiter in the club just for to open the door?"

"Yes; but—"

"And another just for to lick the stamps? My!"

"William leaves the club at one o'clock?" I said, interrogatively.

She nodded. "My mother," she said, "is one to talk, and she says Mr. Hicking as he should get away at twelve, 'cause his missis needs him more'n the gentlemen need him. The old woman do talk."

"And what does William answer to that?"

"He says as the gentlemen can't be kept waiting for their cheese."

"But William does not go straight home when he leaves the club?"

"That's the kid."

"Kid!" I echoed, scarcely understanding, for, knowing how little the poor love their children, I had asked William no questions about the baby.

"Didn't you know his missis had a kid?"

"Yes; but that is no excuse for William's staying away from his sick wife," I answered, sharply. A baby in such a home as William's, I reflected, must be trying; but still—Besides, his class can sleep through any din.

"The kid ain't in our court," the girl explained. "He's in W., he is, and I've never been out of W.C.; leastwise, not as I knows on."

"This is W. I suppose you mean that the child is at West Kensington? Well, no doubt it was better for William's wife to get rid of the child—"

"Better!" interposed the girl. "'Tain't better for her not to have the kid. Ain't her not having him what she's always thinking on when she looks like a dead one?"

"How could you know that?"

"Cause," answered the girl, illustrating her words with a gesture, "I watches her, and I sees her arms going this way, just like as she wanted to hug her kid."

"Possibly you are right," I said, frowning; "but William had put the child out to nurse because it disturbed his night's rest. A man who has his work to do—"

"You are green!"

"Then why have the mother and child been separated?"

"Along of that there measles. Near all the young 'uns in our court has 'em bad."

"Have you had them?"

"I said the young 'uns."

"And William sent the baby to West Kensington to escape infection?"

"Took him, he did."

"Against his wife's wishes?"

"Na-o!"

"You said she was dying for want of the child?"

"Wouldn't she rayther die than have the kid die?"

"Don't speak so heartlessly, child. Why does William not go straight home from the club? Does he go to West Kensington to see it?"

"'Tain't a hit, it's an 'e. Course he do."

"Then he should not. His wife has the first claim on him."

"Ain't you green! It's his missis as wants him to go. Do you think she could sleep till she knowed how the kid was?"

"But he does not go into the house at West Kensington?"

"Is he soft? Course he don't go in, fear of taking the infection to the kid. They just holds the kid up at the window to him, so as he can have a good look. Then he comes home and tells his missis. He sits foot of the bed and tells."

"And that takes place every night? He can't have much to tell."

"He has just."

"He can only say whether the child is well or ill."

"My! He tells what a difference there is in the kid since he seed him last."

"There can be no difference!"

"Go 'long! Ain't a kid always growing? Haven't Mr. Hicking to tell how the hair is getting darker, and heaps of things beside?"

"Such as what?"

"Like whether he larfed, and if he has her nose, and how as he knowed him. He tells her them things more 'n once."

"And all this time he is sitting at the foot of the bed?"

"'Cept when he holds her hand."

"But when does he get to bed himself?"

"He don't get much. He tells her as he has a sleep at the club."

"He cannot say that."

"Hain't I heard him? But he do go to his bed a bit, and then they both lies quiet, her pretending she is sleeping so as he can sleep, and him 'feard to sleep case he shouldn't wake up to give her the bottle stuff."

"What does the doctor say about her?"

"He's a good one, the doctor. Sometimes he says she would get better if she could see the kid through the window."

"Nonsense!"

"And if she was took to the country."

"Then why does not William take her?"

"My! you are green! And if she drank port wines."

"Doesn't she?"

"No; but William, he tells her about the gentlemen drinking them."

On the tenth day after my conversation with this unattractive child I was in my brougham, with the windows up, and I sat back, a paper before my face lest any one should look in. Naturally, I was afraid of being seen in company of William's wife and Jenny, for men about town are uncharitable, and, despite the explanation I had ready, might have charged me with pitying William. As a matter of fact, William was sending his wife into Surrey to stay with an old nurse of mine, and I was driving her down because my horses needed an outing. Besides, I was going that way at any rate.

I had arranged that the girl Jenny, who was wearing an outrageous bonnet, should accompany us, because, knowing the greed of her class, I feared she might blackmail me at the club.

William joined us in the suburbs, bringing the baby with him, as I had foreseen they would all be occupied with it, and to save me the trouble of conversing with them. Mrs. Hicking I found too pale and fragile for a workingman's wife, and I formed a mean opinion of her intelligence from her pride in the baby, which was a very ordinary one. She created quite a vulgar scene when it was brought to her, though she had given me her word not to do so, what irritated me even more than her tears being her ill-bred apology that she "had been 'feared baby wouldn't know her again." I would have told her they didn't know any one for years had I not been afraid of the girl Jenny, who dandled the infant on her knees and talked to it as if it understood. She kept me on tenter-hooks by asking it offensive questions, such as, "'Oo know who give me that bonnet?" and answering them herself, "It was the pretty gentleman there;" and several times I had to affect sleep because she announced, "Kiddy wants to kiss the pretty gentleman."

Irksome as all this necessarily was to a man of taste, I suffered even more when we reached our destination. As we drove through the village the girl Jenny uttered shrieks of delight at the sight of flowers growing up the cottage walls, and declared they were "just like a music-'all without the drink license." As my horses required a rest, I was forced to abandon my intention of dropping these persons at their lodgings and returning to town at once, and I could not go to the inn lest I should meet inquisitive acquaintances. Disagreeable circumstances, therefore, compelled me to take tea with a waiter's family—close to a window too, through which I could see the girl Jenny talking excitedly to the villagers, and telling them, I felt certain, that I had been good to William. I had a desire to go out and put myself right with those people.

William's long connection with the club should have given him some manners, but apparently his class cannot take them on, for, though he knew I regarded his thanks as an insult, he looked them when he was not speaking them, and hardly had he sat down, by my orders, than he remembered that I was a member of the club, and jumped up. Nothing is in worse form than whispering, yet again and again, when he thought I was not listening, he whispered to Mrs. Hicking, "You don't feel faint?" or "How are you now?" He was also in extravagant glee because she ate two cakes (it takes so little to put these people in good spirits), and when she said she felt like another being already the fellow's face charged me with the change. I could not but conclude, from the way Mrs. Hicking let the baby pound her, that she was stronger than she had pretended.

I remained longer than was necessary, because I had something to say to William which I knew he would misunderstand, and so I put off saying it. But when he announced that it was time for him to return to London,—at which his wife suddenly paled, so that he had to sign to her not to break down,—I delivered the message.

"William," I said, "the head waiter asked me to say that you could take a fortnight's holiday just now. Your wages will be paid as usual."

Confound them! William had me by the hand, and his wife was in tears before I could reach the door.

"Is it your doing again, sir?" William cried.

"William!" I said, fiercely.

"We owe everything to you," he insisted. "The port wine—"

"Because I had no room for it in my cellar."

"The money for the nurse in London—"

"Because I objected to being waited on by a man who got no sleep."

"These lodgings—"

"Because I wanted to do something for my old nurse."

"And now, sir, a fortnight's holiday!"

"Good-bye, William!" I said, in a fury.

But before I could get away Mrs. Hicking signed to William to leave the room, and then she kissed my hand. She said something to me. It was about my wife. Somehow I—What business had William to tell her about my wife?

They are all back in Drury Lane now, and William tells me that his wife sings at her work just as she did eight years ago. I have no interest in this, and try to check his talk of it; but such people have no sense of propriety, and he even speaks of the girl Jenny, who sent me lately a gaudy pair of worsted gloves worked by her own hand. The meanest advantage they took of my weakness, however, was in calling their baby after me. I have an uncomfortable suspicion, too, that William has given the other waiters his version of the affair; but I feel safe so long as it does not reach the committee.

www.ingramcontent.com/pod-product-compliance
Lightning Source LLC
Chambersburg PA
CBHW050921120626
46552CB00004B/1700